The Eyes
of a
Wolf

A Zev Evans Novella

James
LePore

THE
ST●RY
PLANT

The Story Plant
Studio Digital CT, LLC
PO Box 4331
Stamford, CT 06907

Story Plant Paperback ISBN-13: 978-1-61188-250-6
Fiction Studio Books E-book ISBN-13: 978-1-945839-07-8

Visit our website at www.thestoryplant.com
Visit the author's website at www.jamesleporefiction.com

First Story Plant Paperback Printing: February 2017

Printed in the United States of America

I dedicate this book to the memory of
Everett, Mary, and John Chandler.

CHAPTER 1

I should have started with Carol, not Grace, but just the thought of writing the Carol story flattened me for a week. When I got up, I started writing the Grace story. Actually, I googled "how to write a story" first, which also flattened me, but only for a day. It might be obvious to anyone with half a brain that googling "how to write a story" is a foolish thing to do, but I was desperate and very anxious. And though Carol did her best, I am pretty sure that I actually do have only half a brain, maybe even less. With that much brain missing you'd think I'd be a person with a mental disability, but I'm not, not in the traditional way at least. (I am way behind everybody else when it comes to keeping up with which words are currently forbidden, and which are allowed. I mention this because I was going to use the word "retarded," but something told me to be careful. Sure enough, my Google search told me that it's offensive, although at one time it was considered a polite way of saying "moron" or "imbecile." I'm sure "mental disability" will someday soon also be considered offensive. In fact, any word or group of words that are in any way offensive to any human being,, or that differentiate in any way among or between human beings, will eventually be banned. We'll have to resort to numbers as identifiers, but even that could be a problem as many people will see the higher numbers as discriminating against the lower numbers, or vice versa. We'll be in a pickle then, with no permissible words or numbers. What happens at that point is anybody's guess. Perhaps a Forbidden Word Underground Railway will spring up, where people can travel secretly to secret places where they can all shout out forbidden words for an hour or two and then go home laughing or sobbing, or both, at how absurd their lives have become.)

Anyway, whatever parts that shrapnel in Samarra destroyed were replaced by some other stuff that has made me a strange and frightening fellow, even to myself. I have that beast under control now, but if you hire me, I will let him off his leash, and you will be satisfied with the results. The means you don't want to know about.

I digress, which, if you've read *Breathe in Grace*, you know is something I do. If you haven't, you are now finding out. I can control it sometimes, sometimes I can't. You may want to put the book down, or throw it out the window. I understand. You're looking for the story to begin and are frustrated or bored. Just to be clear, when I say flattened, I mean drink until I'm stupefied, feeling nothing, thinking nothing. The only thing I feel when I'm in that state is the plate in my head. I mean literally feel it sitting up there. I have an X-ray of it on the wall in my kitchen, so I know what it looks like, too—rectangular and curved, like somebody cut out a piece

of a soccer ball. There must be some strange iso-
topes in it, because when Carol put it in, whatever I
could do before, I could do much, much faster after.
This includes bad things, like worrying or letting
my thoughts get away from me, or wandering off
point, like I'm doing now. Also, repeating myself,
so if I say something here that I said in Grace's story, I apologize. Of course, you may not have read
Grace's story, so this will all be new to you. That's
a conundrum that I guess writers who write stories about the same characters have. There's more
to writing than I thought, but, as you can see, I'm
forging ahead.

Back to Carol.

It was nine years ago. Carol had left the Army
and was doing brain surgery in Los Angeles. I was
living in my mother's house, drinking, smoking,
and running all over Long Island trying to kill the
Tasmanian devils leaping around inside my head
like monkeys on speed. (I know what a metaphor
is, but do tend to mix them. This one is at least con-
sistent in that it refers to animals and doesn't mix
them with something else, minerals for example, or
vegetables). I had gone to live with my mother in
Glen Cove when I was discharged from the Army
in 2004. My mother, a full-blooded Sicilian from the
high hill country near Enna, thought that somebody
had given me the evil eye, so she prayed constantly
for the spell to be broken. She told me that if I drank
in her house, she would throw me out, but then
she'd open a couple of bottles of my grandfather's
homemade wine (to honor and remember him, she
said) and we'd both get drunk and watch Jeopardy

while eating pasta. "What is Heisenberg's uncertainty principle?" she would blurt out, slamming her hand on her Formica-topped kitchen table, a forkful of twirled spaghetti suspended in mid-air and a fierce look in her crazy Sicilian eyes. "Don't mess with me Alex," was one of her favorite lines.

When word came in 2005 that my father had gone missing while on assignment in Lebanon, my mother started wearing black. "How do you know he's dead?" I asked her. I suggested that maybe he was being given a new identity, getting ready for a special operation. The Mossad did this occasionally - faked an agent's death so the top hadjis, the ones who actually thought about things, would stop looking for him, especially an agent as hated as my father was. "I had a dream last night," she said, "he was on top of a building, calling to me, Adalina, Adalina, waving to me to come to him. He's dead."

Two years later, a DHL van appeared at our house. The driver, a Mossad agent, told us that my father had been killed in a car bombing in Beirut in 2005. He did not say why it took so long to tell us. The Mossad did what it did for reasons of its own. The agent gave my mother an envelope with ten thousand dollars in cash in it and paperwork explaining how to access a pension account opened for her in the Cayman Islands. The next day she left to collect my father's remains. Before she left, she gave me the ten thousand dollars the agent had given her and told me to find a place of my own. "Mangia questa minestra, o saltare dalla finestra," she said. Eat this soup or jump out this window.

I am ashamed to say that when my mother got in the cab, I began hyperventilating and passed out on the floor, where I lay inert for an hour or so. Afterward, I called Carol and described what had happened. She didn't think I'd had a seizure, but told me to continue taking my Phenobarbital, which I wasn't taking and still don't, but said I would. Of course, she said to see a local neurologist, which I also said I would do, but didn't. I wish I had listened more carefully to Carol's voice because she was in trouble then, and I might have been able to help her sooner.

When I said running all over Long Island, I meant it literally. Ten miles a day was the average. I would drive to different towns, park my car, and run a figure eight—which, on its side, is the symbol for infinity—through the town. If it was a small town, I did two loops, or three. My goal was to make the figure eight as smooth as possible. This was difficult because as everyone knows, most city and suburban blocks are at right angles. I often cut across lawns to smooth things out. I saw all kinds of people on these runs doing different things, living their lives. I always wished I was one of them. When I was done, I felt normal for a while. You don't know what a blessing it is to feel normal when you've had what a Brit friend of mine in Iraq called "the screaming habdabs" for most of your waking hours for days on end. "It's similar to your heebie-jeebies," he said, when I asked him what he was talking about. After a run and a shower, I could do normal things in a normal manner for a couple of hours. Make coffee. Shop for food. Sit on the deck. Write a poem. You're probably laughing, and I don't blame you. A psycho vet with a plate in his head and a trail of dead and maimed bodies behind him who writes poetry. It's funny of course, but true. I wrote a poem for Carol once, but never gave it to her. I was too embarrassed. As to the maimed and dead bodies, well, that's on the table now.

A couple of days after my mother left, I pulled a groin muscle on one of my runs, dodging a kid on a bicycle who darted across my path. I tried to run the next day, but it got a lot worse. It was a stupid thing to do. With running out of the question, the only thing I could do was drink, so I drank for one whole day. The next morning, my friend Johnny Scoglio found me on the floor of my mother's brocaded living room with her pillowcase full of cash clutched to my chest. Before Johnny revived me, he took a picture, which I also have in my kitchen pinned next to my skull X-ray. It's not a pretty picture, as I had puked and rolled in it face first like a hungry dog.

"Carol Harris has been trying to reach you," Johnny said, handing me one of the prepaid cell phones he used at all times. "She's in trouble."

CHAPTER 2

I used some of my mother's money for an open-ended round trip ticket and was in Los Angeles the next afternoon. Actually, Johnny used his credit card to buy my ticket as I did not have a credit card then, and buying airline tickets with cash was not a smart thing to do because of 9/11. Because of the plate in my head, I have a special pass that gets me through airport security, though airport security is mostly for show anyway. They were frisking a white-haired old lady wearing those crazy oversized glasses that old people wear when I went through. She looked like a creature from outer space. Just who you want your government to profile.

I drove around Los Angeles in my rented car until I found a neighborhood I liked the look of, which is to say, bleak. I passed a Days Inn and a Starlight Hotel and then spotted the Queen of the Angels Motel on Valley Boulevard in a neighborhood I later learned was called El Sereno that was as unhip and un-Hollywood as you can get. There was a carwash next door on one side and a boarded up building with seagulls painted on it on the other. Across the street was a one-story windowless building with ten or twelve overflowing trash cans on the curb, a sure sign of endemic dreariness. Vacant lots are also highly reliable evidence of bleakness, and there were plenty of them around as well. I checked in and called Carol on one of the two prepaid phones Johnny gave me when he drove me to the airport. I knew nothing back then about how cell phones could be hacked and tracked with ease if you knew what you were doing, but when it came to this type of stuff, I always took Johnny's advice and still do. Some people call these phones "burners," but I think "throwaway" is more precise because you throw them away after using them once which prevents tracking. Actually the throwaway can still be tracked, but you are far gone.

My call to Carol went to voicemail. *"I'm here,"* I said and gave her the phone's number. I figured she was working, drilling into someone's skull, so I changed into jeans, a T-shirt, and sneakers, sat under a sagging trellis, and listened to the Top 40-type tunes that were being piped into the motel's center courtyard. In the middle of the courtyard was a small, fairly clean pool surrounded on all sides by the two-story motel. All the rooms faced the pool. The concrete apron around the pool was painted a bright pink with graffiti covering a lot of it. Most of the graffiti consisted of names spray-painted in primary colors. I spotted *Cadillac Jack, Franny and Zooey* inside a heart, and *james22@gmail.com* among them. There were half a dozen plastic chairs strewn around the apron. This was in October, and the weather was beautiful. I didn't think much about why the pool was devoid of people, but learned later that the Queen didn't come alive until late at night when the drug dealers, pimps, and hookers that lived there came out to socialize after their night's work. I was nervous sitting there, but the music calmed me enough so that I could be still and think a little bit. I'm a lot better now, but in those days, moments of clarity were rare. While I was sitting, I went over my conversation with Carol.

"Did you have a high school sweetheart?" she asked, with no preliminaries, as if the answer was such a big deal she had to blurt the question out before getting to anything else. Like, *How are you Zev? How's your head? Are you taking your pheno?* I remember looking down at the dried puke on my shirt and thinking, *What happened?* Which is what I said.

"What happened?"

"Did you?"

"Yes," I answered. "Did you?"

No answer. I could hear Carol breathing.

"Yes," she said, finally.

"What happened?"

"He didn't wait for me."

"Who?"

"My high school sweetheart."

"Carol…"

"I married someone else."

"I thought you were single?"

"When I got home."

"From Germany?"

"Yes."

"Is that good or bad?"

"Bad."

"What happened?"

"Can you come out here?"

"Of course."

"Tonight?"

"What's going on?"

"Can you?"

"I'll come tomorrow."

"I'll tell you when I see you. But first, tell me what happened with your high school sweetheart."

"She died in a car crash on the night of our senior prom."

"Oh, Zev," Carol said. "Zev…"

"It's okay," I said.

o o

My girlfriend (her name was Angela Rossi) told me at the prom that she was pregnant and that she was getting an abortion the following week. I didn't try to talk her out of it. I was so stupid at the time, it didn't occur to me that she was mad at me. She was Sicilian (like one-half of me, the other half is Jewish) from a strict family. I should have known. The slightest scrutiny of her face would have told me. But stupid is stupid, especially at eighteen. She left with some girlfriends, saying she would meet me at a kid's house that we knew in the Hamptons. I was sitting on a dune behind that kid's house drinking a beer at seven in the morning when a long shadow appeared over my shoulder. I turned and saw my father, who was home on one of his brief visits. When he saw me, he turned and went back to the house to call my mother. They told me later they thought I had died in the same crash as Angela. I didn't tell my parents that Angela was pregnant. At least I saved them that.

I also tried to join the IDF, which I thought would be easy as I am an Israeli, as well as an American, citizen, but my father, who was an Israeli war hero, blocked it. As a consolation, he placed me unofficially with a group of recruits in the IDF's special forces training camp in the Sinai after I graduated high school. Over six hot months I learned the basics of commando warfare, including how to organize hostage rescue, sabotage, and hit-and-run actions. I could fire my Uzi on semi- or full automatic with either hand and with great precision. I also became highly proficient with the Beretta Jaguar pistol they issued me. I was so good that after I completed the training, the IDF asked my father if I could join a counterterrorism unit that was being formed at the time to clean out a nest of Hezbollah rodents in southern Lebanon. He agreed. Of the twenty people in the unit, ten were killed (two of them were women) but we destroyed a missile base along with about fifty rodents. My father then insisted that I come home to watch after my mother. This is a job he abdicated many years before, but she never complained, and I never knew him well enough to get angry or bitter.

I still train with the newest versions of the Beretta Jaguar. It's like sailing or golf, training with my weapons, it calms me and keeps my mind off of my problems while I'm doing it. I've never sailed or played golf, but this is my take on why people do these things. If I'm wrong, you can pick any activity you like that fits the picture. To this day, I live by one simple rule when confronted by an enemy: attack.

When I came home, I worked on construction for a while and then joined the NYPD. That didn't work out, (I explained why in *Grace,* so I won't repeat it here) but the silver lining is I met Johnny at the Academy, and we're still good friends. Johnny is now the world's premier computer hacker, something that only he and I, and his commanding officer at the NYPD's Counterterrorism Bureau know.

CHAPTER 3

The woman who had checked me in at the front desk brought me a drink while I was sitting under the trellis. I was immediately unnerved as she was only half-dressed in a halter top and shorts, and, though I had tried not to make it look obvious, I had stared at her when I was checking in. She had told me her name was Eva.

"You look like you could use a drink," Eva said.

The drink had a paper umbrella sticking out of it. The swizzle sticks had angels on top. Mine had half its head missing. Eva brought herself a drink too, and sat down at my table. Plastic angels, most of them deformed, were spread out among the purple bougainvillea that covered the trellis. Some were hanging by a leg, others had their heads missing or no wings. They looked as if they had been attacked by a force of bigger angels and left in disarray. The shadow of one of these angels, one with only one wing, fell directly on Eva's chest.

"I do?" I said.

"You've been sitting here for two hours staring at the pool."

"It calms me," I said.

"The pool?"

"Yes."

"Why do you need calming?"

"What's in the drink?" I asked, for something to say. *Why do you need calming?* What kind of question is that? I remember thinking at the time. I hadn't said *I need calming,* I distinctly said *it calms me.*

"Rum, mostly," she said. "I just pour different shit in."

"You're not a board certified mixologist?"

"No, and I don't fuck for money."

I nodded, as if this was something people said to each other every day, like, I don't shop at Costco or I hated algebra, and took a sip of the drink. It was okay, but anything would have been. I didn't care much how drinks tasted in those days and still don't.

"Are you here on business?" she asked.

To have someone talk directly to me like that was disconcerting, but I managed to say yes in a grim, businessman-like way, or so I thought.

"Where are you from?" she asked.

"New York."

"I'd like to go there."

I nodded again thinking that sounds reasonable. I had a habit in those days of assessing things that people said based on whether it sounded reasonable or not. I was hung up on the issue of reasonableness. Insane, I know. I mean, who sets the standard of what is reasonable or not? I'm over it now, but I still have tics. I think my tics got into my head while Carol was doing my surgery. They were gathered up near the ceiling of the operating room and flew in when they saw their chance. I will try to suppress them as they are boring and will distract from the story, but sometimes I can't, so there's another reason for you to quit now.

"Here," she said, handing me a card with her name and number on it. "Eva Lopez," I said, looking at the card.

"*Si*, and you are?"

"Zevon Evans."

"Zevon?"

"It's Hebrew for wolf."

"Really?"

"Yes."

"I am named after the first woman."

"In Hebrew, it means life." I don't know why I said this. I wasn't showing off. It must have been the shadow floating on Eva's cleavage. The breast angel.

"If I can help you," she said, smiling, nodding at the card.

"Help me with what?"

"Your business."

I will tell you straight out that I am not a handsome guy. I keep my hair long to cover my surgical scar and also because the top of my head is a little lopsided from the loss of bone. I am constantly checking to see if my hair is covering this deformity. Also, if I get anxious when someone is talking to me, especially a woman, I feel a tremendous urge to look away. I fight this, but it sometimes leaves me looking sideways at people, with my head tilted at a slight angle. This of course makes people think I'm weird. It's better now, but if a woman looked at me back then, I began to panic, so I tried not to stare at them, which wasn't so easy as I am a normal male. Eva had taken the card out of the top of her blouse, from in between her breasts, which is where I had been staring. I remember thinking that if she caught me, I'd say I was staring at the breast angel, maybe remark on how charming it was.

"Do you like what you see?" Eva said.

"I..."

"What?"

"I..."

"You can look."

I said nothing. I must have turned a deep shade of red.

"But you can't touch."

"I..."

I had said "I" three times, stopping short each time. After the third time, Eva looked at me carefully, her eyes serious.

"What?" I said.

"You are *timido*."

I wanted to nod, but kept my head still. That's not the half of it, I thought.

"Shy," said Eva.

"I speak Spanish," I said.

"I was teasing." She said this in Spanish, (*Me estaba tomando el pelo*) but I'm translating for you.

"That's okay," I said. I took another quick look at her cleavage. I felt like a Peeping Tom, but I couldn't stop myself. Then again, she said I could look.

Eva smiled and looked at me and took my hand across the table. Now I was really freaked out. My phone rang, which required me removing my hand to pick it up and answer it. It was Johnny calling to find out how I was doing and what was going on.

"Nothing," I said, "she hasn't called."

"How long?" Johnny asked.

"Two hours plus."

"You should go see her."

"I don't know where she lives."

"What hospital does she work at?"

"USC."

"Hold on."

I looked at the pool in the bright sunlight. I had stood up and stepped away from Eva to take the call. Out of the corner of my eye I could see her sipping her drink, looking at me.

"She's not at work," Johnny said when he came back on.

"How do you know?"

"I hacked the HR department."

"That fast?"

"Yes."

Johnny once tried to explain to me what he does, the *0days, OTR's, libpurples,* and other weird things he deals with. It was all over my head. But this stuck: all software is pieced together by normal human beings - that is, flawed, like everyone else. They are thought of as really smart, but they're not. They all leave holes—some small, some gaping—in the programs they design. It is these holes that hackers find and enter. Johnny, who looks like every father or husband who goes to the hardware store on Saturday morning—in fact, he does go to the hardware store on many a Saturday morning— doesn't talk much about other hackers, but as far as I can tell, after working with him for nine years, he is the Superman of hackers. There is no software program he cannot breach, no security system he cannot disable. In 2007, when this story takes place, his job title at the NYPD was *Assistant IT Specialist*, but he had shocked his bureau chief with what he could do and how fast he could do it. He was, at the age of twenty-five, de facto in charge of all internet intelligence gathering for the department. If you don't think this is a big job, just talk to any New York cop or firefighter who was on duty on 9/11.

"Can you get her home address?" I asked Johnny.

"I have it."

He gave it to me.

"Z," Johnny said.

"What?"

"She's on a leave of absence. Her husband called last night."

"Leave of absence? How long?"

"Indefinite."

"Why?"

"Medical."

Fuck.

"Thanks."

I clicked off and turned to Eva. "I have to go," I said.

She nodded. "You have my card."

I nodded, not knowing what to say. She had an agenda, but everyone does. And she was sexy. She had me thinking about things I hadn't thought of in quite a while. Sex, for example.

"What about the drinks?" I asked.

"Forget it," she said. "On me."

"Thank you," I said. "What do you do here?"

"I run the place."

"Who's watching the front desk?"

"Nobody. We don't get a lot of walk-ins. There's a bell that rings out here. You're the first one to use it in six months."

"You have a selective clientele."

"You could say that."

"Like Franny and Zooey."

"They're back in Guatemala now."

I nodded. I had read all of Salinger and thought that that particular graffito was a sly joke of some kind, but apparently it wasn't.

"I wasn't coming on to you," Eva said.

I was confused. Then I remembered she had reached out to touch my hand.

"I was trying to get a reading."

"What?" I said. "Are you a psychic?"

"Sometimes."

I nodded. *Who was this woman?*

"Try breathing," she said.

"What?"

"Breathe in something good, breathe out something bad."

CHAPTER 4

I was twenty-seven then. I was going to stay in the Army for as long as they'd have me. I wasn't good at anything except the fighting part, but in a war zone, that's all that matters. In the field, that is, which is where I was mostly. We seemed to always be at war somewhere, so I felt I had a shot at a long career. It didn't work out. Driving from the motel to Carol's house, I thought about my behavior since getting home. Disgraceful. And now the woman who had saved my life was sick, so sick she wasn't able to pick up her phone and call me. I got even more depressed when I got into Pacific Palisades. The houses were big, and there was a beautiful sunset over the Pacific, but something didn't feel right. This wasn't Carol, these mansions and all this pretentious bullshit. I was shocked actually. Don't get me wrong, I really didn't know much about Carol at the time. When I woke after my surgery, she was sitting on the side of my bed holding my hand. She did that twice a day until I was sent back to the States. What doctor does that? She told me a little about herself, where she was from, etc. I told her what I could remember about myself. It was mostly quiet sitting, five or ten minutes at the most. I don't think I even thanked her properly. I was spaced out from the head injury and the surgery, but that's no excuse. Both my parents told me never to make excuses for my own failures. I doubt I will ever have kids, but if I do, I would tell them the same thing.

I didn't have time to analyze my feelings of shock (*Why wouldn't a successful neurosurgeon live in a big house with an ocean view? What's so shocking about that?*) because as I was parking, a beefy guy in a white shirt and very dark sunglasses came out of Carol's house and walked over to my rental car. As I put my window down, he pulled out a nine-millimeter pistol, chambered a round, and pointed it at my head, then casually tilted his sunglasses up to look at me from under them. He hadn't shaved in a few days, and I could see hair growing out of his nostrils. A bandito type. He gave me a smirky look, and was about to speak, but before he could, I knocked him down by opening the driver side door very hard into him. Very hard. So hard that when I got out to check on him—he was lying face up on the street—I thought he might be dead. He wasn't. The gun had landed a few feet behind him. I grabbed it and hit him on the side of the head with it. I went through his front pockets, which were empty.

As I was turning him over to get to his back pockets, two more guys in dark glasses and white shirts came out of Carol's house. When they saw what was going on, they drew weapons, which was a mistake. I shot them both in the forehead with the smirky bandito's gun. I wiped the gun down with my T-shirt, placed it in his right hand, put his index finger on the trigger, and fired a round in the direction of the house. I didn't know how much good this would do as the cops would surely wonder how he managed to get knocked out after killing two guys, but it was the best thing I could think of. Maybe they'd think he got hit by a car, which then fled.

I should have taken the dead guys' wallets, but I felt an urgency to flee, which I did. The gun was a Glock 25, which makes enough noise to be heard in the nearby houses. They were widely spaced semi-mansions, acoustically engineered to keep the outside world as muffled as possible, but I wasn't taking any chances. I did take a second to scan the nearby light posts for surveillance cameras, seeing none. At first I thought I might abandon the car and report it as stolen, but the lies I would have to tell to the rental company and possibly the cops seemed much too complicated, so I drove to the airport and turned the car in. On the way, I threw my number one prepaid phone out the window. I used the second one to call Eva to ask if she could pick me up at the airport. She said she would for fifty bucks. I told her I'd give her a hundred.

CHAPTER 5

I threw the second phone away, too. You're probably thinking I was paranoid, which I was, extremely. I mean, the beefy guy who needed a shave, why did he pull a gun on me? I was just a citizen parked across the street from Carol's house. I could have been anybody. He knew I was coming, that's why. How? I had called Carol twice, once from Long Island on one of Johnny's throwaways, the second time from my motel on my number one prepaid phone. The first time we talked for a few minutes, the second time I left a message. Someone was listening in on Carol's calls. Someone traced my route from my motel to Carol's house via the battery signal from my first phone. The smirky bandito was obviously expecting me. When Eva picked me up, I asked her to take me to the nearest Radio Shack, where I bought four more burners under various fictitious names.

I should mention that driving to the airport, I was in a bit of a state of shock, not to mention awe. Not at what I had just done, but at how I felt about it, which was really good, really excellent. Three years ago, Carol had given me my life back, but the thing is, it was a crappy life, me getting drunk all the time, passing out, throwing up. It wasn't hard to connect the dots. I was a soldier again. *Bang, bang,* one guy maimed, two dead. I wasn't ready to swear off drinking, but this was better. And cheaper. I hadn't even used my own gun.

"Where to now?" Eva asked when I came out of the Radio Shack.

"I can't go back to the motel," I said.

Eva nodded. She didn't ask why, which I didn't focus on at the time, but when I thought about it later, I realized was an amazing thing. What person, especially a woman, wouldn't ask *why* in a situation like that?

"I need my things though," I said.

"I'll get them for you."

"And pay my bill?"

"Sure."

"How much do you want?"

"What else do you want me to do?"

"I need a place to stay. I need a gun and ammunition."

"Anything else?"

"A car. A knife, duct tape."

"A hundred a day, plus expenses."

"You'll be my assistant."

"Yes. Strictly professional. No sex."

"Did I say anything about sex?" I said. "You've got sex on your brain."

"Ooh, *mi amado,* you are sexy when you're angry."

"Why are you calling me your darling?"

"How about *Papi?*"

I didn't answer. What do you say to something like this?

"You're angry," Eva said.

"I'm not angry."

"If you say so."

I pulled out my wallet, took ten hundred-dollar bills out of it, and gave them to Eva. She put them down her blouse, the yellow halter.

"Where are you taking me?" She had gotten onto a freeway.

"My house."

"Are you going to charge me?"

"Now you insult me."

I thought about her offer. I had just maimed one guy and killed two others in broad daylight. All three had come out of Carol's house. I was going back there, but I needed to get out of sight at least until dark. I had my mother's ten thousand dollars with me, less the money I had given Johnny to buy my plane ticket and the thousand I had just given Eva. I could check into a cash-only, no-questions-asked flophouse, but those places are full of snitches and various other types of lowlifes, happy to sell me out for twenty bucks. Plus, anywhere I went, I'd have to take a cab or have Eva drive me. Witnesses were everywhere, and, even then there were cameras, everywhere. (Now, nine years later, we're all being videotaped all the time. I would suggest to anyone interested that they keep this in mind as they go about their lives.)

"Okay," I said, "but just until I can get a car."

"Whatever you say, *Papi*. By the way, if anybody asks, I'm Mexican."

"You're not Mexican?"

"No, Cuban."

I decided not to ask her why she was trying to pass for Mexican. Being with her was starting to get a little complicated. All these curve balls.

"Who might ask?"

"My neighbors."

"I'm not moving in."

"They're nosy."

"If you hadn't told me you were Cuban, I would have assumed you were Mexican."

"Why?"

"I'm a bigoted, insensitive, white American male. All Hispanics look alike to me."

"Yes, but you are very beautiful, especially when you're angry."

"I'm not angry, and I'm definitely not beautiful."

CHAPTER 6

Eva lived in Boyle Heights behind a church with a painting of Jesus on one wall and Our Lady of Guadalupe on the other, on either side of the front door. Her house consisted of a kitchen, a sitting room, and a bedroom, right in a row, each room slightly smaller than the other. From the outside, it looked like a large toy telescope. I sat at her wooden kitchen table, which was next to a large bay window that looked out onto the street, and called Johnny on one of my new burners. I asked him to immediately check for any police activity on Carol's block in Pacific Palisades and to see if there were any cameras within a thirty-block radius. He called me back in fifteen minutes to say the answer to my first question was no, and that the nearest camera was on a pole in a shopping center a mile away.

"Did you go by that?" he asked me.

"No."

"What's up, Z?"

"I don't know. I don't think Carol's sick."

"What happened on her street?"

Johnny had four kids, a great wife, and a good life. Whatever phone he used was secure, but I wasn't worried about surveillance. People were dead. I had killed them, and I was pretty sure there were more to come, especially if someone had hurt Carol in any way. Helping me put Johnny's whole life in jeopardy.

"I'm involved already, Z," Johnny said.

"Not really."

"I'm coming out there."

"No, you're not."

"I'm not kidding. Toby never asks any questions. If you don't tell me, I'll get on a plane tonight."

Toby was Toby Howard, Johnny's bureau chief, a hard-bitten Jew who knew that Johnny was a genius, with skills the best hackers only dreamed of acquiring. Anything Johnny wanted, he got, anything he wanted to do, including fly away for a week or two, he could do. Johnny's people were from Calabria, the southernmost region of the Italian mainland. Calabresi were more hard-headed than most Sicilians. A baseball bat would not make a dent in their heads. I hated doing it, but Johnny and I were now a team.

"Okay," I said. "I left a guy on the street with some broken ribs and a gash on his temple, a big one."

"Dead?"

"No. And two other guys."

"What about them?"

"Immobile."

"In the middle of the street?"

"In front of the house."

"How immobile?"

"Dead."

"You didn't take any cell phones, I hope? They can be tracked."

"No."

"Nothing's been reported."

"Are you sure?"

"I hacked into the LAPD's Comm Center. Everything's recorded. Nothing."

"Can you keep checking?"

"Of course. Easy."

"Thanks."

"Z…"

"Yes."

"You sound different."

"I'm doing a special op."

Silence, then, "Really?"

"Yes."

"Are you still staying at the same motel?"

"No."

"Where?"

"I made a new friend."

"Really?"

"Really."

"Who?"

"Her name's Eva Lopez. I'm staying with her."

"What's going on?"

"I don't know, but I'm about to find out."

In Iraq, guys wanted me with them on patrol for various reasons. One of them was my shooting skills. Another was my very quick reflexes. But something had changed on Carol's street. *You sound different*, Johnny had said. He didn't know the half of it. Those three guys at Carol's house were all Mexican, in their mid-twenties, the fat one about five-eight, two hundred pounds. The other two, the dead ones, a little taller, about a hundred and fifty pounds. Anybody could see this, but one of the dead ones had a two-inch scar on his left cheek, the other had something wrong with one of his eyes. It seemed half closed. I saw these features clearly in the second or so it took to lift the gun, take aim, and fire. I hadn't gone to the range in nearly a year. If I had thought about it beforehand, which I didn't, I would have expected my reflexes to be slower, and my aim to be off. But I had gotten better, not worse. I was willing to bet that my shot placement with a semi-automatic pistol was now in the center of a one-half inch square target at or close to a hundred feet. I felt like I was about a foot away when I shot those two guys. This is not normal. Not even a Navy Seal from a stable stance with a two-hand grip could do this. I was not a Navy Seal, just a regular dog soldier. I did not have the time to question this stuff then, but this I knew: If some private actor had cleaned up that scene at Carol's house, then he was no ordinary bad guy. And I, though I am a neurotic fuck with a plate in his head and beset by odd and sometimes disturbing thoughts, was apparently no ordinary good guy.

CHAPTER 7

It was the guy I hit with the car door, the beefy guy, who gave me my first opening. Johnny found a match to his injuries in the ER and admissions records at USC hospital, the same hospital where Carol worked. The patient, Mauro Salamanca, listing Carol's address on Serenity Road in Pacific Palisades, had been brought in by his brother, Pedro, who said he had fallen from a ladder. Pedro wanted to take Mauro home, but, as he was unconscious, the hospital refused, citing California law. Something told me the alleged brother would not take no for an answer, so I borrowed Eva's car and drove to USC. At the front desk I said I was Mauro's other brother, Carlos. I peeked into the room before entering and saw Mauro asleep, hooked up to an IV and some kind of brainwave monitor. At least that's what I assumed it was. It could have been fake for all I know, a false front, like a movie set. How do we know any of those gadgets in hospitals are real? It could all be part of a game hospitals play, where people either die or get better on their own, no matter what the hospital does, which is probably true half the time anyway.

There was a chair pulled up to Mauro's bed with a light jacket draped over the back. I went in, moved the chair to the other side of the bed, picked up a metal water pitcher, and went into the closet. Mauro's visitor—loving brother Pedro I assumed— returned a few minutes later. He was a bit confused at first, but then sat down with his back now to the closet. I stepped quietly out and hit him on the head with the pitcher as hard as I could. He went down like a fallen tree. I took his wallet and phone. In the closet, I found Mauro's clothes hanging neatly, and his personal things—a wallet, a cell phone, and a large silver and turquoise ring—in a drawer. I took his wallet and phone as well. I took Mauro's picture and Pedro's with my phone. I went out through the front door. There were security cameras in the lobby, at the front desk, and in the parking garage, but Johnny had disabled them all.

In the parking lot, per Johnny's instructions, I called him from Mauro's and Pedro's phones and hung up after each call went to voicemail. I then wiped the phones down and chucked them into some shrubs. Having the numbers of these phones, Johnny could find out where they were purchased and what other numbers they had been talking to. You are probably as surprised as I was at the time that Johnny could do these things. I have since learned not to be surprised at anything he does. Frodo and those guys had Gandalf. I have Johnny.

CHAPTER 8

When I got back to Boyle Heights, Eva went out to get me the things I had asked for. While she was gone, I called Johnny. He had already tracked Mauro's and Pedro's phones, which he told me were both bought in August in electronics stores in Tijuana. The calls made from these phones were all to other burners, whose numbers Johnny tracked to the same stores. No ID is required to buy prepaid phones in either Mexico or the US, so this was a dead-end. Undaunted, Johnny told me to take pictures of everything in Mauro's and Pedro's wallets and email them to him, along with the pictures that I had taken of them, which I did. When this was done, per his instructions, I packaged the two wallets to overnight to him. While I was putting them in an empty cookie tin I found on the kitchen counter, a black cat with big yellow eyes came out of Eva's bedroom and sat on the striped rug that covered most of the kitchen floor and watched me. I knew nothing about cats in those days and was a little spooked at first. When I was done, he jumped onto the table and rested a paw on the back of my right hand, sort of in the same way Eva did when I first met her at the Queen of the Angels Motel.

Later, Eva told me he was taking a reading. As you probably know by now, it is never a dull moment with Eva.

Eva was back in an hour with a Beretta M9, ten fifteen-round magazines, five boxes of ammo, a belt holder for two clips, a car from a local chop shop with California plates registered to a dead guy in Pasadena, and a friend named Diego, who had driven the chopped car. In the glove compartment of the car were a half dozen plates registered to six other dead guys, along with a stiletto and two rolls of duct tape. The plates she thought I might need, which was good thinking on her part. I had hired a self-starter. Diego was the nephew of the pastor at Our Lady of Guadalupe, the church in front of Eva's house. He lived in a room in the attic and was the groundskeeper and a deacon there. His uncle, the pastor, was visiting relatives in Mexico. "He went home to die" is how Diego put it. Once a month, a priest from another church would come and hear confessions on Saturday and say mass the same evening. Otherwise, Diego, who also served as the visiting priest's altar boy, was alone and in charge.

Diego offered to come with me to Carol's house. He was young, maybe nineteen, slightly built, and definitely gay. I declined. Another person, especially someone I didn't know, would be a burden. Johnny had told me not to go to Carol's until we knew who we were dealing with, but I knew who we were dealing with: three guys who tried to kill me and now a fourth guy with a cracked skull. Not them, specifically, as two of them were dead and the other two decommissioned, but whoever else might be at Carol's house involved in whatever it was they were doing that was serious enough to try to kill me. Diego, who did not seem offended by my refusal of his offer to help, told me the quickest way to get to Pacific Palisades, which was basically the 10 to the coast. Not Route 10, or just 10, but *the* 10, which is how they say it in California, which is how I am saying it out of respect for the local culture.

CHAPTER 9

When I got to Carol's house, there were two vehicles in the circular driveway, a van and a Mercedes SUV. I turned off my car's lights and parked
across the street. I couldn't stay long. This was a
rich neighborhood with no other cars parked on the
street, which meant someone was sure to call the
cops. One drawback of being rich is that you have
to be diligent about guarding your money and your
property. This may not sound like a big deal, but I
have a feeling it can be nerve-racking. Poor people
don't have this problem. They have others, but not
this one. I was about to get out and approach the
house when two bandito types came out dragging
Carol between them. They were followed by a tall,
thin guy with long, dark, flowing hair. He had on
a dark sport coat with an open-collared white shirt
under it. It was dark, but I would recognize Carol anywhere. She is a farm girl from Kansas with
freckles and blue eyes and yellow hair. The banditos shoved Carol into the van, and the hip-looking
guy got in the Mercedes. I followed them with my
lights off until we were on the 405, then turned
them on. The license plates on both vehicles were
covered in mud or streaks of dark paint.

CHAPTER 10

Two hours later, about ten miles from the Mexican border, the van and the Mercedes exited the freeway onto Dairy Mart Road. The sign said SAN YSIDRO/IMPERIAL BEACH. We drove through a shabby residential area and on into the night for another ten minutes or so. About a mile past a sign that said, WELCOME TO THE TIJUANA RIVER VALLEY WHERE BIRDS FLY AND PEOPLE DIE, they turned onto a long dirt driveway, and then a few minutes later into the front yard of a small one-story house. I had turned my lights off when we got off the freeway. I stopped well back and watched the van park in front and the two banditos pull Carol out and enter the house. She was totally limp, a rag doll. The Mercedes pulled around to the back. I watched its taillights disappear into the black wasteland that surrounded us. A light came on in the front of the house. This threw off enough light for me to read the sun-bleached sign in the front yard of the house that said, PRIVATE PROPERTY. I was parked next to a ditch filled to the brim and higher with old tires that someone had tried to burn and that still stunk. When the wind shifted, I could smell raw sewage. I have smelled a lot of bad things in my life, but these two combined were gag-inducing.

I could have stayed parked there all night if I wanted to, but that wasn't my plan. I could easily get in a window and take out the two banditos, but then Carol might get caught in a crossfire. Also, I wanted one of them alive. I would worry about the Mercedes later, improvise if he came back. I stuck the stiletto in my pocket, got out, drew my Beretta, and circled around back. Through a dirty window I could see the two banditos at the kitchen table drinking tequila. No Carol. There was a back door with a washing machine on cinder blocks next to it. Next to the washing machine was a rusted propane tank. I rapped on the door, then nestled between the washing machine and the propane tank. One of the banditos came out with a gun drawn. Light from the kitchen spilled in a sort of cone shape into the weed-and-rubble-filled backyard. The other bandito said from inside, "*Que pasa?*" They were clichés speaking in clichés. The first bandito muttered something in reply. I could have easily shot him, but I didn't want to make any noise, so I tapped on the side of the propane tank with my pistol and watched as he turned and walked toward me. When he got close enough, I grabbed him by his head, broke his neck, and laid him gently on the ground. In my head, no time passed between me jumping out, or rather, thinking of jumping out and him being dead on the ground. It probably took about two seconds. But as I said, for me, no time passed. He's alive, he's dead, that's it. In a sense, he was dead before I killed him. If you can understand that, call me, because I can't.

Bandito number two now called out again, "*Que pasa, Carlito?*"

"*Salido*," I said, making my voice rough like I was drunk. "*Te necesito.*"

"*Que pasa?*"

"*Nada, necesito una bebida.*"

"*Ah, si, muy tequila.*"

They were both drunk, so I never had any worries. I was just fucking with number two. When he came out, the thick and squat Patron Silver bottle in his extended hand, I took it from him and clubbed him with it. For good measure, when he was down, I smacked him in the temple with the barrel of my Beretta.

Carol was out cold on a pile of old blankets in a closet-sized room next to the kitchen. I carried her to my car and laid her on the back seat. Then I went back and taped up bandito number two's mouth, hands, legs, even eyes and ears, and dragged him to the car and threw him in the trunk. I fished his phone out of his pants pocket and threw it in the shit-and-tire-filled ditch.

I went back again to see what I could find in the house. On the kitchen counter I found a pharmacy vial with no label with about twenty yellow and white gel pills in it. On the yellow side were the letters LV, on the white, the numbers 901. I put it in my pocket. In the back was a big room, maybe twenty by twenty feet. I kicked through some old blankets, raising a cloud of dust and the smell of urine. Under one blanket I found a photo of a dark-haired, dark-eyed family—mother, father, and two kids, a boy and a girl. The father had a dirty bandage on his head, and one of his eyes was purple and swollen shut. I put the picture in my back pocket. As I was turning to leave, I thought I saw movement in a corner. It was dark in the room, but my eyes had adjusted. I pulled out my Beretta, chambered a round, and approached the corner. A blanket moved, and then a small head appeared from under it and looked at me. It was a child with big dark almond-shaped eyes, matted stringy black hair, and a filthy face. A girl. I wrapped her in the blanket, picked her up, and went back to the kitchen, where I washed her face with tap water. At first she thought I was going to drown her, and she resisted. I told her I was just going to wash her face. She let me, then rested her head on my shoulder. I made a cup out of my right hand, poured some tap water in it, and motioned to her to drink from it, which she did, like a kitten. She weighed less than my gun. I grabbed two bottles of water from the fridge, the cleanest dish towel I could find, a chair cushion, and left.

In the car, I laid the child, who was awake but very still and weak, on the front seat. I then cleaned up Carol's face and neck, which were filthy, and dribbled some water onto her lips and a little in her mouth. As I was laying her head on the cushion, she opened her eyes and looked at me.

"Zev?" she said.

"It's me."

"I can feel the breeze ..."

"I can, too," I said.

"Is it you?"

"Yes, it's me."

"Are you okay?"

"Yes, I'm okay."

I was about to say more, but she had already fallen back to sleep.

I drove up to the house, got out, and took a few pictures of it, front, back, and both sides to send to Johnny. In back, as I was backing up to get the whole house in my phone's lens, I stumbled on something. When I looked down, I saw a cement cap the size of a manhole with a metal ring in the center. I pulled the cap off expecting to smell sewage, but only smelled dank air. There were wooden steps descending into blackness. I put the cap back.

My eyes were adjusting to the darkness, so I decided to take a quick look around before leaving. A few yards away I spotted fresh tire tracks leading into the desert, which I followed. I was worried about Carol and the kid alone in the car by the ditch, but the guy in the Mercedes looked like a boss to me, and I very much wanted to talk to him and then probably kill him. After about fifty yards, I heard a noise that sounded like a garage door opening and closing. I crouched behind some scrubby bushes and watched as the boss guy got in the Mercedes, which was parked next to a trailer, and drove off into the night. When he was gone, I made my way to the trailer. It had a huge padlock on it, which I blew off with my M9. I swung the door up and saw the cargo, about thirty Mexicans. Some of them had water bottles in their hands. All of them were filthy. They all looked like they were in shock, like zombies in a bad movie.

I still had my gun in my hand. I waved it toward the desert.

"*Ir,*" I said. "Go."

CHAPTER 11

"Who is she?" Eva asked.

"Carol Harris," I said. "She's a friend of mine, a doctor."

"And the guy in the trunk?" she asked.

"He was holding her prisoner."

"The little girl," Eva said, "must have belonged to the people in the trailer. The coyotes must have forgotten her, left her behind."

"Who?"

"The coyotes."

"Who are they?"

"I will tell you, but first I need to know the whole story."

"Even if I've killed somebody?"

"Yes."

"Why?"

"I work for you. I am an accessory, a *coconspirador*. I am entitled to know."

We were sitting at Eva's kitchen table with a bottle of tequila between us. She was dressed the same as before, a yellow halter top, shorts, and three-inch cork wedges with rhinestone studs on the straps. Diego had gone to the church to get clothes for Carol and the child from the donor bin in the basement. Carol and the girl were in Eva's bedroom with a woman named Janine, a nurse practitioner. I poured us each about an inch and a half of tequila.

"Drink first," I said.

We downed the tequila.

"I have a plate in my head," I said. "Carol put it in. She's a brain surgeon. It's from shrapnel when I was in Iraq. She called me yesterday and asked me to come out. She was in some kind of trouble." I looked at my watch. It was 3 a.m., so technically she had called me two days ago. Not technically, actually.

"What kind of trouble?"

"She didn't say."

"She's a mess."

I nodded.

"So?" said Eva.

"That's the thing," I said. "I don't know much. I'm waiting for my friend in New York to get me some information."

"Is that the package I sent?"

"Yes. And I emailed him some other stuff. Pictures I took tonight."

"You won't get nothing on the guy in the trunk."

"Why not?"

"He's scum, a guard dog. The lowest of the smuggling gangs."

"Smuggling gangs?"

"Yes. They bring drugs and *illegales* over the border. You don't know what a coyote is?"

"Not the animal, I'm sure."

"Where you been?"

"Iraq for two years and then drunk for three years."

"A coyote smuggles people across the border. He knows the best trails, the best places to stop. Scouts go ahead and look out for border patrol."

"How do you know?"

"That house where you found your friend?"

"What about it?"

"It's a stash house. The coyotes lock up the *illegales* there, then demand extra money. Sometimes they put them in trailers and move them around the desert. They burn them with cigarettes or cattle prods and then send pictures to their families in Mexico. Rival gangs raid each other's stash houses all the time."

"How many gangs are there?"

"Who knows? There are turf wars. I hear two right now. There were three, but there was a shootout in Tijuana last week. One gang was eliminated."

"There was a manhole in the backyard."

"A tunnel is the safest way across. The border is right there."

"How much do they get?"

"A thousand, two thousand, more sometimes."

"Per person?"

"*Si.*"

"How many come across?" I asked.

"I don't know, thousands, many thousands."

I pondered this.

"Your friend is pretty. *Muy bonito. Como un ángel.*"

I nodded. When I first saw Carol, I swore her yellow hair was a halo. I was in a fugue state from the injury and the surgery at the time, seeing double. My head soon cleared, and my vision got better, but that's how I always thought of her, as an angel.

"*Tu ángel?*" Eva said.

"No," I said. "It's not what you think."

Eva nodded. "*Bueno.*"

While we were waiting for Janine, Eva had cleaned Carol and the child as best she could and given the child a small glass of warm milk and a cookie.

"Did you see the needle marks on her arms?" Eva asked.

"No."

Needle marks. I poured myself another drink and one for Eva. We both drank quickly. As we were putting our glasses down, the bedroom door swung open, and Janine came out. She sat down at the table with us. Eva got up and got her a glass.

"How is she?" I asked.

"Who are you, *senor*?" Janine asked.

Before I could answer, Eva put the glass down, perhaps a little too sharply, and said, "He is my friend. You are in my house."

"And her? Who is she?" Janine said, tilting her head in the direction of the bedroom.

"My friend as well," said Eva. "She's visiting."

"And the child?"

"Her daughter," said Eva.

"What happened?"

"I told you, she passed out."

The women, both in their primes and good-looking, sexy Latinas, exchanged hard looks.

"How is she?" I asked again.

"Drugged, but okay," said Janine, turning back to me.

"What kind of drug?"

"Probably a barbiturate."

"What did you do?"

"I gave her something to counteract the sedative. I hooked up an IV. She's dehydrated."

"She'll be okay?"

"Yes. Her vitals are okay. She just has to sleep it off."

"How long will she be out?"

"It's hard to say. A few hours, maybe more. It depends on the dose."

"And the child?" I asked.

"Malnourished. Feed her. Slowly."

"What do we owe you?" I asked.

"A hundred," said Janine.

I gave her a hundred-dollar bill.

Eva poured us all drinks, and we drank. When we were done, Janine got up.

"I'm going," she said.

When she left, the cat came in and sat on the chair that Janine had been sitting in.

"What's his name?" I asked.

"Nero."

"Black?"

"Yes."

"Not the emperor?"

"Emperor?"

"A Roman guy. He fiddled while Rome burned."

"In Cuba we learned only communist history. All bullshit."

"He touched me when you were out."

"He was taking a reading."

"Did he tell you his findings?"

"He confirmed that you are a good guy, but very neurotic. *Muy neurótica.*"

"He's wrong."

"I don't think so."

"I've killed three guys since I've been here. Just so you know. Did Nero know that?"

"He doesn't talk."

I shook my head. *Eva.*

"I'm going over to talk to that little asshole in my car."

"You won't get nothing out of him."

"Why not?"

"I told you, he's just a guard dog, an *illegale* like the rest, stupid, no English, drunk half the time."

"How do you know?"

"The *jefes* are too smart. He won't know anything."

"I'll try."

"How?"

"I don't know."

"You're not a torturer. Besides, you have Carol. You've saved her."

I hadn't thought of torturing the guy, just asking him a few questions, then killing him no matter what his answers were. I admit, I was in a state of bloodlust after seeing what had been done to Carol.

"I want to know," I said, "who told him to take Carol to the stash house."

"He gets a call. That's all he knows. A voice tells him what to do. If he doesn't do it, his family will be killed."

"He must have met somebody."

"He was probably recruited in Tijuana. A guy at a bar. No name. The guy gives him a dozen cheap phones. One phone per week for twelve weeks. When the phones run out, a stranger gives him twelve more, or they kill him and dump his body in the desert. With the money he makes, his family lives well. Until they get rid of him."

"How do you know all this?"

"All Mexicans in L.A. know these things."

"But you're not Mexican."

"I'm passing. I might as well be."

"What do we do with him?"

"He didn't see you?"

"No."

"Put him on the street. He'll survive. Or he won't."

I nodded my agreement. Eva had saved the guy's life.

"Eva, I left two guys dead and another maimed on the street in front of Carol's house tonight. There's been no report of it, which is very odd. It means we are dealing with the worst kind of people. I will leave and take Carol with me if you want."

Eva did not hesitate. "No," she said. "We have made a deal. And I need the money."

CHAPTER 12

I drove bandito number two to a vacant lot in Watts, which I'd always wanted to see. I am a ghetto aficionado. I'm not sure why. Maybe it's because they're different countries, not part of the United States. I don't doubt the Crips and Bloods will start issuing passports one day soon. I would if I were them. Dawn was breaking, which meant that if they were anything like their counterparts on the East Coast, the gangbangers would all be home sleeping off whatever they had consumed last night. No respectable gangbanger is out past 2 a.m. The time between 2 a.m. and 5 a.m. is for assassins and other professionals. I had a lot of vacant lots to choose from. I chose one on a side street, checked for cameras, and opened the trunk. My bandito was awake now, but not struggling too much. I pulled him out and for a moment considered untying his hands so he could get the tape off of his feet, mouth, and eyes. I am, after all, a good guy according to Nero, who doesn't talk. But I didn't. I didn't want him getting lucky and seeing my car and license plate, even though it was completely bogus. I threw him in some weeds and drove off.

On the way back to Eva's, Johnny called to tell me that the L.A. police had dispatched a patrol car to Carol's house last night in response to a call from a Nicolas Castillo reporting that he had returned home from a business trip to find that the alarm system and security cameras at his house had been disabled and that his wife, Carol Harris Castillo, who had been ill, was missing. The house off of Dairy Mart Road was owned by N.C. Holdings, a California corporation that owned a few hundred acres of played out farmland on the Mexican border in the Tijuana River Valley. The IDs I sent him from the Salamanca brothers—California driver's licenses—were fake, decent forgeries. There was no match to their pictures. He had received the wallets a few minutes ago from FedEx. He would have them dusted for prints, but he wasn't optimistic.

I asked Johnny to get me what he could on the gangs that smuggled illegals across the border from the Tijuana area into California. I was particularly interested in the names of the leaders.

"There's something else," Johnny said.

"What?"

"Nicolas Castillo is a Los Angeles City Councilman. And Carol Harris is the sole shareholder of N.C. Holdings."

CHAPTER 13

There was a mud-caked Mercedes SUV parked in front of Eva's house when I got back there. Its license plate was covered with mud. The front door was unlocked. Eva and a thin Hispanic guy about my age, with long, dark, flowing hair, were sitting at the kitchen table drinking coffee. The door to the bedroom was open.

"My friend Zev," said Eva, introducing me.

"Ricky Marquez," the man said, nodding. I watched as he assessed me.

"Zev Evans," I said.

"Did you get your cigarettes?" Eva asked.

"Yes," I replied, tapping my shirt pocket.

"Detective Marquez is looking for a woman named Carol Harris Castillo," said Eva.

Marquez took a pack of Marlboro reds from an inside pocket of his hiply unconstructed blue blazer, extracted one, and handed it to me.

"Do you know Senora Castillo?" he asked. He lit my cigarette and one for himself, ignoring Eva, which I felt was rude, though I was pretty sure she didn't smoke.

"I met her in Germany," I answered. "She operated on my brain." I had been trying to quit smoking since I got home from Iraq, but the first drag reminded me why I was having so much trouble doing it. It also reminded me of Iraq, where I smoked incessantly, which is not a bad thing. I liked it there. There's nothing, I will add, apropos of nothing, like a Marlboro red at five in the morning to remind you of life's ultimate struggle—to simultaneously defy death and embrace it.

"Your brain?"

"Cracked skull, acute subdural hematoma. Trephination of the head."

"You're not from here?"

"No."

"Where?"

"Glen Cove, New York."

"What brings you here?"

"The surgery, or the injury, I'm not sure which, left me with special powers."

"Special powers?"

"Special powers."

"I can arrest you right now, Senor Evans."

"For what?"

"Obstruction of justice."

"She called me," I said. "She said she needed my help."

"With what?"

"Picking out new drapes."

"Have you seen her?" Marquez smiled, but I could see his heart wasn't in it.

"No," I replied.

"Where are you staying?"

"Here," said Eva.

"What brings *you* here?" I asked Marquez.

"Have you seen Senora Harris?"

"I told you, no."

"I always ask twice. It gives people a chance to examine their conscience."

"Assuming people have a conscience."

Marquez didn't try to fake a smile this time.

"So you have not been to her house?"

"No."

"Do you know where she lives?"

"No."

"She can't be such a good friend."

"She's not," I said, "but when someone opens up your skull cavity and looks in, it creates a bond for life."

Marquez crushed out his cigarette, taking his time, then looked at me. I could tell he wasn't happy, though he was trying to be cool.

"Do you have a warrant?" I asked.

"Eva gave her consent."

"Do you want to hear about my special powers?"

"No."

"I'm good with guns."

"I hope you are not looking for trouble, Senor Evans."

"Because I'll find it?"

"Yes, you will. The *senora* may have been abducted. For that you get twenty years in California."

"Where in California?"

"You are trying to be cool, funny perhaps," said Marquez. "Perhaps to anger me. It won't work. I am very careful about my emotions, especially when I'm working."

"I apologize," I said. "I'm worried about Carol."

"Her husband is worried, too. A neighbor thought he heard gunshots near her house yesterday. On the street."

"Gunshots?"

"Yes."

"Were there shell casings? Cartridges? Any forensics?"

"We don't talk about open investigations."

"I'd like to help."

"No, *senor*, you should go home. We will find her."

"Okay," I said, "but you know what they say in the Marines."

"What do they say in the Marines?"

"No better friend, no worse enemy."

"Is that a threat?"

I shrugged. "Can I have your card?"

"Eva has it. Do not leave Los Angeles, Senor Evans. I may want to talk to you."

"Sure thing," I said, nodding. "By the way, detective, didn't I see you tonight?"

"See me? Where?"

I waited a beat to let Marquez think this over.

"At the 7-Eleven on Marango," I said.

Marquez had been looking at me with keen, but disdainful interest. Now his look changed.

"You were buying water," I said. "Five cases. I thought, there's a guy who drinks a lot of water. Or knows a lot of thirsty people."

"No," he said. "Not me."

"I said to myself, now there's a handsome guy, a Marc Anthony look-alike."

Silence.

"The singer?" I said.

You know the old saying? If looks could kill? If they could, I'd be dead.

CHAPTER 14

"Where are they?" I asked Eva when Marquez was gone.

"In Diego's car, driving around."

"What happened?"

"We were having coffee. We heard him pull up and looked out. Diego carried her and the child out the back. He keeps his car behind the church."

"What about the IV?"

"Under the bed."

I shook my head. This was not good.

"Janine," I said. "How well do you know her?"

"I…"

"What?"

"She is the only one who will come to a house around here. Your friend was unconscious. You said no hospitals. We had no choice."

"But you don't trust her."

"No."

"Why?"

"She treats illegals. Cleans their wounds, gives them shots. They're afraid to go to the emergency room or to see a real doctor. For twenty dollars, Janine will do what she can."

"So?"

"She knows them, she knows where they're living. She has power over them."

"Does she use it?"

"She acts like she's their friend, but we think she has turned some in."

"Great. Did Marquez ask about the coffee cups?"

"Yes. I told him a friend was staying with me."

"Me."

"Yes. But he seemed to know about you."

"Why do you say that?"

"The way he smiled when I told him."

"What's Janine's last name?"

"Gutierrez."

"She must have made a call as soon as she left. Do you know her number?"

"Yes."

"Write it down."

Eva dug an old supermarket receipt out of her purse, wrote on it, and handed it to me. I texted it to Johnny: *Who has she been talking to?*

"We were lucky," I said. "But he'll be back."

"*Si.*"

"We're a good team, Eva…"

"*Pero?*"

"Tell me the truth. How do you know so much about the smuggling gangs?"

"People in the neighborhood," she said.

"What about them?"

"I have put them in touch with people. To get relatives across. They trust me."

"For a fee."

"Yes."

"How much?"

"Three hundred dollars."

"In touch with who? What people?"

"A guy I know who will bring people across and not fuck them over."

"Who is he?"

"He's dead."

"How do you know?"

"His wife called to tell me. He was killed in the shootout I just told you about."

"Last week."

"Yes. I think Janine placed her finger on Juanito."

"Placed her finger?"

"Turned him over. Turned him in."

"I see. Who's Juanito?"

"My coyote friend, the one who's dead now."

"Sounds like a dangerous business," I said.

Eva nodded and was quiet for a second. Then she said, "Zev?"

"Yes?"

"I thought I was doing a good thing, helping people get across."

Silence. In which Eva's big dark eyes softened and then quickly hardened. In that instant I saw an Eva I hadn't seen before, an Eva with memories she'd rather not have.

"You were," I said.

"What should we do?"

"Marquez could have taken you in," I said. "He had direct evidence from an informant. You're a material witness. I think his visit was unofficial."

"Unofficial?"

"I think he's working for someone, maybe the same people that cleaned up the scene on Carol's street."

"That can't be good."

"You'll have to move, hide someplace," I said. "He'll pick you up if he gets frustrated."

Eva nodded. "There's more," she said.

"What?"

"Marquez knew I was illegal, he threatened me."

"Illegal? I thought Cubans could stay once they touched American soil."

"I stabbed somebody in Cuba."

"Stabbed somebody? Who?"

"A government inspector who tried to rape me. I grabbed a kitchen knife. I can't go through the process for the green card. They will send me back. Castro does not forgive."

"Did you kill the guy?"

"I don't know. I left him bleeding and ran. It doesn't matter, I will be executed."

"How did you get out?"

"We had a raft hidden on the beach, for emergencies."

"How old were you?"

"Fourteen."

"How did he know you were illegal?" I asked.

"I don't know. He's a cop. They know things."

"He won't bother you anymore," I said.

"How do you know?"

"I know."

CHAPTER 15

"I have an idea," said Eva.

"I'm listening."

"There's a doctor who sometimes comes to the Queen. I think he's debarred. He's a drunk, but he comes."

"The Queen?"

"Your motel, your ex-motel."

"Debarred?"

"*Inhabilitado.* Fired from being a doctor."

"And?"

"He treats the whores and the junkies."

"Whores and junkies?"

"They live there."

"Can you contact him?"

"Yes."

"I will kill that *puta*," said Diego.

We were sitting in Diego's car, behind Our Lady of Guadalupe. Carol was asleep in the back seat, still out cold, her head in Eva's lap. The child, also asleep, lay curled up between me and Diego on the front seat. Eva had called Diego when Marquez left, and he came back to the house to pick us up.

"Let's go," I said.

CHAPTER 16

"Zev."

"Carol." I squeezed her hand.

"Where am I?"

"You're safe."

"Who's that watching television?"

"A Mexican kid."

We both looked across the room to a small sitting area where the little girl was watching *Family Guy*, a show I had never seen but am now hooked on.

"What's her name?"

"I don't know."

"Let's ask her."

"She won't talk."

"Won't talk? Why? Where am I?"

"At a motel in El Sereno."

"I don't understand."

"You were drugged. Do you remember calling me?"

"Yes, I do. When was that?"

"Two days ago. You said you were in trouble."

Carol nodded. She looked tired and pale, but she was okay. Eighty-year-old Sid Bernstein, El Sereno's disbarred alcoholic doctor to the decrepit, had revived her.

"You said you'd tell me about it when I got here," I said. "What's going on?"

"My husband..."

"What about him?"

"I think he tried to kill me."

"How?"

"I found some papers, a corporation in my name, all the stock."

"N.C. Holdings."

"Yes. N.C. Holdings. I asked him about it. He said it was an investment he made, it was going to be a gift to me. I called our accountant. He said N.C. Holdings owned property in San Ysidro. He said he thought I knew about it. I had signed papers."

"You didn't."

"No."

I squeezed her hand again. Looking at her—blonde, freckles, light blue eyes, a neurosurgeon who sat and held her patients' hands after surgery—I was ashamed of myself. What right did I have to be on the same planet as her?

"I had a high school sweetheart, too," Carol said. "I should have married him."

"You told me."

"My husband..." She looked down, then back up at me.

"What happened?" I asked.

"The accountant must have called Nick. That night after dinner I had a tremendous headache. I called you. After that it's a blank."

"The doctor said you were given a barbiturate. Probably crushed in your food. Then an injection. Do you remember anything about last night?" I had shown Dr. Bernstein, ex-doctor Bernstein I should say, the yellow and white capsules I had taken from the house on Dairy Mart Road, which he immediately identified as Nembutal, forty milligrams.

"No," Carol answered.

When I told Bernstein about how long and how deeply Carol was out, he surmised that someone had given her another shot of a narcotic of some kind in the last few hours. There were two needle marks on her left arm. This was probably Janine Gutierrez. She was now on my list. There were others ahead of her, but I would get to her.

"I found you," I said, "and took you to a friend's house and then here."

"Found me where?"

"San Ysidro."

"What doctor?"

"Sid Bernstein. Do you know him?"

"No."

"He treats the losers of the world, being one himself."

Carol smiled at this. "I have to call the hospital," she said.

"Your husband already did. He said you were sick and would be out for a while. Leave it at that."

"Where's my phone? People will be calling me."

"Your husband probably has it. He's probably answering calls, bullshitting your friends."

"I should call them."

"No, you shouldn't, absolutely not."

"What should I do?" she asked.

"Stay here. My friend Eva runs the place. She's moving you to a building next door, a closed up bar that used to be part of the place."

"Why?"

"People are looking for you. Your husband has a detective working for him."

"The child, too?"

"Yes. Eva will take care of you both."

"How long?"

"Until I do what I have to do. It won't take long."

"Zev?"

"Yes?"

"You saved my life."

"No," I said, "you saved mine, again."

"I don't understand."

"I'll explain later."

I remembered the photo of the Mexican family in my pocket. I took it out and gave it to Carol. We both looked at it and then at the child watching TV. The girl in the picture wasn't her.

"Who is this?" Carol asked.

I shook my head, thinking of the people in the trailer who Marquez had brought water to and then locked them back in.

"Carol," I said. "Your husband's a bad guy."

"I know. I've known it for a while. I'm sorry I got you involved."

"Don't be, you did me a favor."

"I did?"

"I've found my calling."

CHAPTER 17

"We got lucky," Johnny said.

"How?" I asked.

On the crappy butt-burned desk in my room at the Queen was a map of the San Ysidro area with Dairy Mart Road highlighted in yellow. The house where I had found Carol was circled in red marker. It was about a hundred feet from the Mexican border. Next to the map was a satellite picture with a red circle around a house in Tijuana under construction. The image was so good you could see a corner of one of the tarps covering the roof curling up in the wind. Next to the house was a half-full dumpster. The map and the satellite picture came to me via email from Johnny. I had printed them out in the motel office and called him, as he asked me to do.

"The prints," Johnny replied, "on one of the wallets you took from the guys in the hospital match a guy who was deported last year. He ran into a school bus with his pickup. He was drunk. One kid was killed, eighteen were hurt."

"Which wallet?"

"Mauro."

"So he went to jail and then got deported?"

"No jail."

"How can that be?"

"Don't ask me."

"They let him back? He killed a kid."

"They didn't let him back. He just came across."

"Who's they, by the way?"

"ICE. U.S. Immigration and Customs Enforcement."

"There's more to this border crossing thing than I thought."

"You've been out of it, Z."

That was an understatement.

"Not anymore," I said. "What's his name? The kid killer?"

"The one he gave to ICE was Jose Maria Ibarez."

"What about him? He's gone now."

"The address he gave ICE is in the Castillo neighborhood in Tijuana."

"Let me guess, the one under construction?"

"Yes. My ICE contacts tell me it's a common tactic. Take off the roof, punch out new window openings. It's cover for building a tunnel. The dumpster carts away the debris and dirt."

I looked at the map. I didn't realize how close to the border I was that night on Dairy Mart Road. The tunnel to the stash house would be no more than three hundred feet.

"The Castillos were one of the founding families of the city," said Johnny.

"Carol's husband's name," I said.

"Right. The house under construction is owned by a lawyer in Mexico City."

"What kind of lawyer?"

"He represents the Tijuana cartel people."

"Drugs."

"Yes, and recently people."

"What's his name?"

"Roberto Castillo. He's Carol's husband's brother."

"What did you get on him, the husband?"

"He owned porn shops in L.A., then sold them about five years ago and started a development company, buying land and trying to develop it. That's when he went into politics. The development company went bankrupt two months ago, but he's very popular, a champion of all things Latino. He and Carol got married last year."

"All things Latino?"

"The city is half-Hispanic. If you count the illegals, it's probably sixty percent. In ten years, it'll be eighty percent."

"What about Marquez?"

"He was a beat cop five years ago. Now he has a gold shield."

"So Castillo is his rabbi?"

"Castillo is the chair of the city council's police relations committee. So yes, he must be."

"Any word from Serenity Road?"

"Nothing."

"Is ICE getting involved?" I asked.

"They want the tunnel destroyed, but they'd need a warrant. You'd have to sign an affidavit."

"Do they know about me?"

"No."

"Leave it that way. I'll take care of it."

"Can I help?"

"What kind of explosives do the Mexican cartels use?"

"I'll find out."

"Thanks."

Johnny was silent for a moment.

"Don't ask," I said.

"I won't. When do you need to know?"

"Now."

"Okay. Anything else?"

"I may need a delivery of whatever it is."

"Sure."

Another pause.

"You sound good, Z. *Are* you?"

"I'm *muy neurótica*, as Eva says, but yes, I'm fine."

"Be careful," Johnny said.

"I'll be fine."

"*Muy neurótica*," said Johnny. "I like that."

CHAPTER 18

"*Ola,* Ricky."

"*Ola.*"

"I am on Dairy Mart Road."

Pause. I could imagine the expression on Detective Marquez's face. The phone Janine was using, a throwaway, was on the table in front of her, on speaker.

"What are you doing there, Janine?"

"Senora Castillo is here. She needed treatment."

"Who called you?"

"The *gringo,* Zev."

"Is he there now?"

"Yes."

"Can I speak to him?"

"No. He went out to the car."

"So he doesn't know you're calling me?"

"No."

"Give the woman a shot. I will be there in an hour."

"Ricky, she wants to see her husband. She is confused."

"That's not possible, *chica.* Knock her out. I will come and get her."

I nodded.

"Okay Ricky. Shall I stay?"

"Yes, of course. We will stop for a drink on the way back."

"What about the *senora*?"

"We'll take her with us, return her to her husband."

I nodded again, reached over to the phone and clicked the red *End* button. Next to the phone was a roll of duct tape I had used to secure Janine's hands, feet, and neck to a kitchen chair. I put down my Beretta, which I had held to Janine's temple while she talked to Marquez, and picked up the duct tape.

"Do you want to live, Janine?" I asked.

Janine was sweating, the top of her blouse and her armpits were soaked. I had trussed her up pretty good, so she looked like she was in pain as well.

"I know you do," I said before she could answer. "Everybody does. That was a silly question. It was meant to frighten you. Are you frightened?"

"Yes."

"The way the people you prey on are frightened? You and Ricky Marquez."

"Yes."

I fished the vial of Nembutal capsules I had taken from this very kitchen two nights ago out of my shirt pocket, dumped the powder from three of the capsules into a glass of water I had placed on the table earlier, and stirred it with my finger.

"120 milligrams," I said. "It won't kill you, but it will make you easy to handle."

Janine shook her head slightly, which might have been a no, or it might have been involuntary. She had already peed her pants.

"That backpack under your chair?" I said. "There's an IED in it, an improvised explosive device. C-4 attached to a can of ball bearings. The cartels use C-4 all the time, usually in cars, but why not a stash house? They're at war with each other as well as with the cops, aren't they?"

I picked up the Nembutal cocktail, put it to Janine's lips and cupped her chin with my free hand, tilting her head up.

"Drink," I said, "and live. It's up to you."

She drank it down like it was a five hundred dollar shot of tequila.

CHAPTER 19

I parked behind the same pile of stinking tires as I had two nights ago and waited for Marquez. Janine was asleep in the back seat, still trussed up. (I learned in Iraq to take no chances with prisoners). After about an hour, I spotted dust kicking up about a mile away. As his SUV drove by, I could clearly see Marquez's handsome profile. A Latin god, a matinee idol, looking cool, smoking a Marlboro red (unless he changed his brand, which is possible, but my guess is that brand loyalty is very high among Hispanic detectives - *muy fieles a su marca de cigarrillos*). When he passed me, I dialed the first nine numbers of the cell phone in the backpack. At the front door, the detective flicked away his cigarette and went inside. I counted to ten and pushed the button for the last number. Boom. Fireball. Very big fireball. Marquez dead.

Some of the debris from the house landed close to my car.

On the 405, I called Johnny.

CHAPTER 20

"Councilman?"

No answer.

"Councilman sounds so formal. Can I call you Nick?"

No answer.

"It's over, Nick."

"Who are you?"

"Zev Evans, a friend of your wife's. And this is Janine Gutierrez, she's a nurse practitioner." Janine was standing nearby, taking things out of her nurse bag.

"You don't know who you're dealing with," Castillo said.

"Yes, I do."

"What do you want?"

I smiled. I wanted a lot of things, but nothing he could give me.

"A million? Two million?" Castillo asked.

"Your brother's dead," I said. "He was killed in a car accident on the way to work this morning."

No response, but his eyes were a little curious.

"He fucked his own clients."

Nothing.

"Your bodyguards are in a detention center. They were here illegally."

Nothing.

"You and Roberto tried to start your own cartel. You were very stupid. Now he's dead, and you're about to be, too."

"Who are you?"

"Ricky Marquez is dead, too."

"What do you want?"

"You already gave it to me. The night you drugged your wife to keep her from knowing about your new business venture."

Castillo's house was the kind that all rich people live in, big and spacious and beautifully fitted out. We were sitting at the kitchen island, which was as big as most people's living rooms.

"That's a syringe," I said. "And a vial of Nembutal. And latex gloves." Castillo was looking over my shoulder at Janine and the things she had carefully placed on the island's granite countertop.

"You have lots of good reasons to kill yourself," I said. "Shall I go over them?"

"Fuck you."

"I'll take that as a no. But I will say this: Tomorrow, the full story will be in all the papers. How your brother was killed by the Tijuana cartel because he betrayed them by starting a rival cartel, how you killed yourself because, well, it's obvious, you're a crook and a douchebag."

I nodded to Janine, who put on the rubber gloves.

"Would you rather have intramuscular or subcutaneous?" I asked.

No answer. Eyes bulging a bit.

"Never mind," I said. "We already decided on intramuscular. No worries about finding a vein.

You were thinking the same thing, weren't you? That's why you wore your best Gucci form-fitting polo shirt. Easy access to your bicep."

Janine drew the Nembutal from the vial into the syringe, enough, she had assured me, to kill a rhino.

"She won't swab with alcohol," I said. "A person committing suicide wouldn't do that. What would be the point?"

I had tied the councilman-turned-drug-and-people-smuggler's arms, legs, and torso so tight around the five hundred-dollar bar stool he was sitting on that his range of motion was zero. I took the washcloth that Janine had placed on the island and stuffed it into Castillo's mouth. I didn't want him spitting on Janine while she was injecting him. I nodded, stepped back, and then watched as Janine lifted the sleeve of Castillo's shirt to fully expose the left bicep, darted the needle straight in, aspirated for blood (there was none), stabilized the syringe with her left hand, injected the Nembutal, and withdrew the needle. Very professional. After Castillo went limp, which took about thirty seconds, Janine placed the syringe in his right hand and pressed his fingers around it for a count of two, then let it drop to the floor. I untied him, pushed him to the floor, and checked his pulse as a precaution (there was none). I then put the rope in my knapsack, and we left.

CHAPTER 21

Johnny had taken over the surveillance cameras inside the house on Serenity Road, filmed Castillo's execution, then edited the tape to make it appear that Janine had acted alone. He even set up a couple of marks and rehearsed them with me, like the director of a play, to make the editing look perfect, which it did. The video was ready by the time Janine and I got back to the Queen. I showed it to her and assured her that it would be given to the police should she ever again mistreat anyone, try to extort money from her patients, or return to being a paid informant for the LAPD or any other law enforcement agency. Relieved that I had not killed her and having firsthand knowledge of what I was capable of, she consented rapidly.

As far as the world was concerned, Carol had never left her house. Down with a migraine, taking a sedative, she was basically asleep in her darkened bedroom for the better part of three days. When she woke up, her migraine much better, she found Nick and called the police. No, she did not know he was involved in any criminal activities. She was shocked, in fact. Yes, she always kept her physician's bag in her study.

81

After the funeral, the story of the efforts by the Castillo brothers to move in on the Tijuana cartel's business dripped out. There was a shootout in Tijuana recently in which an independent "coyote" was killed, rumor had it, by a Los Angeles police detective. The Tijuana cartel proudly and publicly took credit for the murder of their former lawyer, Roberto Castillo, an obvious warning to their new lawyer. The house under construction in Tijuana's Castillo neighborhood was raided and destroyed by the *Policía Federal*. A house in San Ysidro a hundred feet from the Mexican border, owned by a company controlled by Councilman Castillo, had been blown to bits and a tunnel was found under it. Detective Enrique Marquez was missing, a turn of events deemed to be connected to his close relationship with the corrupt Councilman Castillo.

CHAPTER 22

Carol took a week off after the funeral, during which she found a dozen bank accounts among her dead husband's papers, all in the name of N.C. Holdings, of which she was the sole shareholder. She called her lawyer to ask if she could cash them out, and he said there would be no problem. I drove her around to the different banks. At the end of the bank tour, she had twelve large brown envelopes, each filled with two-inch slabs of hundred-dollar bills, all told over two hundred thousand dollars. After the last stop, she took me to lunch at a place with a walk-up window called Capitol Burgers. We sat at a round picnic table outside and had cheeseburgers, fries, and milkshakes. After our second milkshake, Carol took six of the bank envelopes out of the briefcase she had put them in, along with a small gift-wrapped box, and pushed them across the picnic table to me. I looked down at the array in front of me and then up at Carol.

"If you say no....," she said.

"I won't say no," I said.

"What's in the box?" I asked.

"Open it."

I unwrapped the box, lifted off the top, moved aside the tissue paper, and took out a black T-shirt with *Mangia questa minestra, o saltare dalla finestra* in white block letters across the back.

"Put it on," she said.

"Here?"

"Yes, here, now."

I took off the Glen Cove High School Athletic Dept T-shirt I had put on that morning for my outing with Carol and put on the new one. I didn't even look around to see if anyone was watching. I was concentrating on Carol, who was smiling, which, for the moment, brought all of the ridiculous machinery that spins endlessly around in my head to an abrupt halt. You haven't seen a smile until you've seen Carol's.

"What does it mean?" she asked when I turned around to show her the back.

"Have you been talking to my mother?"

"She called me yesterday."

"You're kidding. How did she get your number?"

"Your friend Johnny gave it to her."

"What did she want?"

"She wanted to know if I had heard from you. I told her we were having lunch today."

The machinery was still shut down. The quiet was amazing. I looked around at the traffic and at the sun shining on Pico Boulevard.

"Your mother told me to say it to you," Carol said. "She made me write it down. I decided to get the shirt made instead."

"It means, *Eat this soup or jump out this window.*"

"Eat this soup?"

"It can be translated various ways, but I know my mother. What she meant was, *Stop whining or kill yourself.*"

"Were you whining about something?"

The machinery started up again. If I could draw a picture of it, it would be of two battered and dirty kids brawling, with curse words like #$!! and #@!* and lightning bolts and daggers shooting out from their heads. Like the old Sunday Newsday cartoons my mother read when I was a kid myself.

"Maybe," I said.

"You didn't tell your mother about your injury, did you?"

"No. Did you?"

"No."

Carol started laughing.

"What's so funny?" I asked.

"She gets right to the point, I guess."

"She does."

"You should call her. She doesn't have the number of your temporary phone, and Johnny wouldn't give it to her. She said he was *balbettio*. What does that mean?"

"He's afraid of her."

"Why?"

"She's part witch."

"Zev…"

"I'll call her when I get to the airport."

Carol reached over and took my hand. The machinery stopped again. She picked up my hand and kissed it.

"Thank you, Zev," she said.

CHAPTER 23

"What's this?" Eva asked.

"Some of Castillo's money," I replied.

She unclipped the flap of each of the brown envelopes on the table in front of her and looked inside. I had written her name on one, Diego's name on another, and Sid Bernstein's on the third.

"Ten thousand for you," I said. "Five thousand for Diego, and one thousand for Dr. Bernstein."

We were waiting for my flight to be called at LAX, at a bar, sitting at one of those high tables where your legs hang down. Through the wall-to-wall, floor-to-ceiling window behind it, we could see large planes being fueled and prepared for their next flight,

"Thank you," Eva said. "*Muchas gracias.*"

"*De nada.*"

"When will I see you again?"

I should have been used to Eva by then, but I wasn't. I felt the blood rushing to my face and sat mute.

"We have to have sex," Eva said.

"Eva…"

"It's your eyes," Eva said. "They are the eyes of a wolf."

"Eva..."

"And your heart," she said. "It is the heart of a lion. What woman would not want to fuck a man like you?"

"Eva, I thought you said..."

"I was playing hard to get. I will come visit you soon."

CHAPTER 24

I was in New York about a month when Carol called to tell me that the girl I had found on Dairy Mart Road had finally started talking. Her name was Isabella. She did not know her last name, nor what a last name was. From what Carol could piece together, with Eva interpreting, the girl was around four or five years old. She had been taken with some other children, by "men with guns," from an orphanage somewhere near a large mountain. Eva would have taken her in hand, but the child clung to Carol, who now wanted to adopt her. I called Johnny, who put Carol in touch with someone who would create an identity for the child, so that she could be easily adopted. Fraud in the service of an innocent child is how Johnny put it.

As for me, I am still *muy neurótica*. I still drink too much, don't sleep much, and have high-octane anxiety much of the time, but at least now I have something to do. Actually, two things to do. One, if you have a problem that the police can't help you with or that you do not have the skill set or nerve to handle yourself, you can contact me, and I will fix it for a fee. Two, I write. The second thing is far scarier to me than the first. Still, I've done it twice now, and I'll probably do it again. No one would know about my writing except I figured out how to self-publish on Amazon. (Actually, after I tried unsuccessfully for about two weeks, Johnny took over and did it in a couple of hours). What consoles me is that my first book, *Breathe in Grace*, is currently ranked 1,101,664 in Amazon's "Paid In" Kindle store. No one's reading it.

As to my fixing business, I have been as busy as I want to be for the past nine years. Eva Lopez is now my quasi-girlfriend and sometimes business partner. You know this if you read *Grace*. If you didn't, now you know. I collect mementos from my cases. I use them as paperweights. Except for the paper ones of course as it would be weird to use paper to hold down paper. I pin the paper ones to my kitchen wall. Among them is a photograph Carol sent me of a graffito: *Carol & Zev*, inside a heart. Someone had spray-painted it on the pink apron of the pool at the Queen of the Angels Motel.

Every time I look at it, I smile.

About the Author

James LePore is an attorney who has practiced law for more than two decades. He is also an accomplished photographer. He lives in Venice, FL with his wife, artist Karen Chandler. He is the author of five solo novels, *A World I Never Made, Blood of My Brother, Sons and Princes, Gods and Fathers,* and *The Fifth Man,* as well as a collection of short stories, *Anyone Can Die* and the collection of flash fiction, *Blood, Light & Time.* He is also the author, with Carlos Davis, of the Mythmakers Trilogy, *No Dawn for Men, God's Formula* and *The Bone Keepers.* You can visit him at his website, www.JamesLeporeFiction.com.